KT-371-972

panda series

PANDA books are for first readers beginning to make their own way through books.

Katie's Caterpillars

STEPHANIE DAGG

• Pictures by Stephen Hall •

THE O'BRIEN PRESS
DUBLIN

First published 1998 by The O'Brien Press Ltd.,
20 Victoria Road, Dublin 6, Ireland.
Tel: +353 1 4923333; Fax: +353 1 4922777
E-mail: books@obrien.ie
Website: www.obrien.ie
Reprinted 1999, 2001.

ISBN: 0-86278-572-3

3   4   5   6   7   8   9   10
01   02   03   04   05   06 07

British Library Cataloguing-in-Publication Data
Dagg, Stephanie
Katie's caterpillars. - (O'Brien pandas)
1. Children's stories
I. Title
823.9'14 [J]

The O'Brien Press receives
assistance from

the arts
council
an chomhairle
ealaíon
50ᴸ

Typesetting, layout, editing: The O'Brien Press Ltd.
Cover separations: C&A Print Services Ltd.
Printing: Cox & Wyman Ltd.

Can YOU spot the panda
hidden in the story?

Katie thought
caterpillars were cool.
Every morning she searched
for caterpillars in the garden.

She talked to them.

She picked them up in her hand
and stroked them.

If she found them on
grotty old weeds, she carefully
lifted them off and carried them
over to **Mum's best roses**.

The caterpillars
loved the roses.
They chomped away merrily.

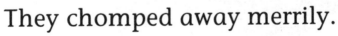

But one day Mum found out
what Katie was doing
and she got very, very cross.

So after that,
Katie left them
where they were.

When it was too wet or too cold to go outside, Katie stayed in and drew pictures of caterpillars.

When she got tired of that,
she painted pictures
of caterpillars.

Then she made models
of caterpillars
out of playdough.

The rest of the time she played
at being a caterpillar and
wriggled around on the floor
– just like a caterpillar!

After a while, Mum got a bit
fed up with caterpillars.
'Would you like a **goldfish**?'
she asked Katie one day.

'There's an old
fish tank in the loft
that you could keep it in.'

'**Goldfish are silly**!'
said Katie rudely.

'Well, how about
a **guinea pig**,
or a **mouse**?'
suggested Mum.
'Or a **kitten**?
Or a **lovely**,
fluffy rabbit?'

'**Yuck**!' said Katie,
even more rudely.

So Mum said no more.

But Katie came to her
a few hours later.
'Mum, I've changed my mind.
I would like a pet,' she said.
'And what would you like?'
asked Mum, amazed.

'A **caterpillar**. Actually,
I'd like lots!' said Katie.

'OK,' said Mum wearily.
'I don't see why not.
I'll go and get that fish tank.
It will be perfect for
caterpillars.'

Katie helped Mum
clean the dust and cobwebs
off the tank.

She watched Mum
make a lid with
lots of holes in it.

They went out to the garden
and put some earth
and grass at the bottom
of the tank.
Then Mum cut off twigs
from different bushes.

Katie arranged them nicely
in the fish tank.

Next she collected
twenty caterpillars
of different shapes,
sizes and colours,
and popped them
into their new home.

Katie was delighted with
her new pets.

She loved each one
and gave it a special name.

There was **Curly** and **Twisty,**
Bendy and **Frisky,**
Greedy and **Stripey** ...
and lot, lots more.

She looked after them
very carefully,
making sure the tank
was kept in a shady place
and finding new leaves
when the old ones were eaten.

The caterpillars got bigger
and fatter every day.

But soon it was time to go
on holiday to Auntie Susan's.
Mum got the suitcases down.
The first thing Katie packed
was **the fish tank**.

'Oh no,' said Mum sternly.
'The caterpillars are **NOT**
coming!'

'But Mum!' protested Katie.
'I can't leave them here.
They'd starve.'

'You'll have to let them go
in the garden then,' said Mum.
'There is plenty of grass
there for them.'

'But they're my **pets**!'
wailed Katie.
**'I'm not throwing
my pets away**!'

'I never said you had to throw them away–' began Mum.

But Katie had rushed off, **howling**.

Mum sighed, and went
to calm her down.
'I've got an idea,' she told her.

Together they went around
to see Mrs Murphy next door.
She was very fond of Katie.
She agreed at once
to look after the caterpillars
while Katie was away.

(Mrs Murphy was so nice
she would look after
a **crocodile** for Katie!)

Next morning
Katie took the caterpillars
to Mrs Murphy's house with
strict instructions on how
they should be cared for.

Then she and Mum set off
in the car. Katie was quite
excited because Mum told her
she might find some
different kinds of caterpillars
in Auntie Susan's garden.
Katie hoped so.

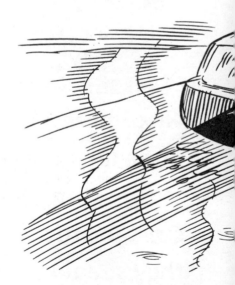

But Auntie Susan put
her foot down.
'There will be **NO**
caterpillar hunting
here!' she said.
'Is that clear, Katie?
You can play with
my kitten instead.'

Katie did not say:
kittens are silly.

She did not say:
I hate kittens.

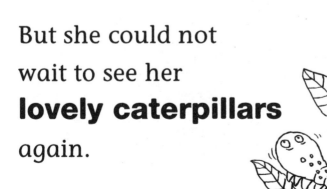

But she could not
wait to see her
lovely caterpillars
again.

Ten days later, Mum and Katie
got back home.
It was late at night
but Katie went to collect
her caterpillars straight away.

She gave Mrs Murphy
a box of chocolates
for looking after them.

She peered into the tank
when she got it back
to her bedroom.
Nothing moved.

'Mum, I can't see
any caterpillars anywhere!'
Katie called.

Mum looked into the tank.
'No, I can't see any either,
but I'm very tired.
Off to bed now.
We'll have a proper hunt
in the morning.'

Katie went to bed –
but she did not sleep.
She got up a couple of times
to look into the fish tank
in the moonlight.
She could see
little wrinkled packages
clinging to some of the twigs.
But definitely
no caterpillars.

Next day Mum was woken up
by a loud scream.
She raced to Katie's bedroom.
'What is it?' she asked.

'Look, Mum, look!'
Katie wailed.
'Look in the tank. It's full of
rotten old butterflies
and they've eaten my
caterpillars, all of them.'
Katie started to cry.

'Oh, you silly thing,'
laughed Mum. 'The butterflies
haven't eaten the caterpillars.
They **are** the caterpillars.'

'You know that caterpillars
turn into butterflies, Katie,
don't you? I'm sure
I've told you about that!'

Katie was horrified.
If Mum had told her,
she had completely forgotten.

How could something
as lovely as a caterpillar
turn into something as
soppy and **daft**
as a butterfly?
In disgust she took
the tank outside.

She watched for a little while
as the new butterflies
dried their wings and then,
one by one, flew off
into the wide world.

Katie had **gone off**
caterpillars.

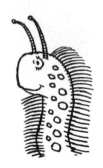

Just then,
a **black**, **shiny beetle**
scuttled across the garden path
in front of her.

Katie stopped.

 She stared.

Then she
smiled.

Beetles were nice
and she knew
for certain that
they stayed beetles ...